Living Things

 HOUGHTON MIFFLIN   BOSTON

Number of Words: 318

Copyright © by Houghton Mifflin Company. All rights reserved.

No part of this work may be reproduced or transmitted in any form or by any means, electronic or mechanical, including photocopying or recording, or by any information storage or retrieval system without the prior written permission of Houghton Mifflin Company unless such copying is expressly permitted by federal copyright law. Address inquiries to School Permissions, Houghton Mifflin Company, 222 Berkeley Street, Boston, MA 02116.

Printed in China

ISBN-13: 978-0-618-75910-1
ISBN-10: 0-618-75910-7

123456789-NCP-12 11 10 09 08 07 06

Contents

1 What Is a Living Thing?

A **living thing** grows
and changes.
It makes other living things
that are like it.
It needs air and food.
It needs water and space.

People and animals
are living things.
Trees and grass
are living things, too.

Nonliving Things

A **nonliving thing** does not eat or drink.

It does not grow.

It does not make other living things that are like it.

It does not need air, food, and water.

living thing

nonliving thing

A nonliving thing may
act like a living thing.
A fire grows.
A fire needs air.
But a fire does not need
food or water.
A fire is a nonliving thing.

Main Idea

What is a nonliving thing?

2 What Do Living Things Need?

Plants and animals need food. **Food** is what living things use to grow.

Plants make their own food.
Plants use sunlight, air, and
water to make food.
Sunlight is energy from the Sun.

Food

Animals eat food.

Some animals eat plants.

Some animals eat other animals.

Many animals eat both plants and animals.
Most people eat both plants and animals.

Food Chain

Plants make their own food.

An insect eats plants.

A bird eats insects.

Water

Plants and animals need water.
Most plants get water
from the ground.

Some animals get water from the food they eat. Many animals get water by drinking.

Air

Plants and animals need air.
Plants use air to make food.
Animals breathe in air.
Whales breathe air
just like you do.

whale

Space

Plants and animals need space.

Plants need space to grow.

Animals need space for a home.

Animals need space to find food.

Shelter

Animals need shelter.
Shelter is a safe place to live.
Some animals find shelter
in trees.

Classify

What do plants need to live?

Glossary

food What living things use to get energy.

living thing Something that grows, changes, and makes other living things like itself.

nonliving thing Something that does not eat, drink, grow, and makes other things like itself.

shelter A safe place for animals to live.

sunlight Energy from the Sun.

Think About What You Have Read

❶ A _____ is a safe place for animals to live.

A) food

B) living thing

C) shelter

D) nonliving thing

❷ What do all living things need?

❸ How are nonliving things different from living things?

❹ Why is sunlight important?